CLARE BEVAN

Make 'em Laugh

Illustrated by Chris Mould

MACDONALD YOUNG BOOKS

Chapter One

Charley was depressed. Very depressed.
It was his ninth birthday. The day he had
dreaded all year.

He trudged up the muddy track in his
comfortable grey uniform and sighed. This
was it then. The end of everything. He was
just the right age to leave Boring Street
Junior School and move on to his parents'
old school.

He gazed down at his neatly laced shoes, his smart trousers, his Boring Street briefcase. Then he took a deep breath and pushed open the caravan door.

The colours dazzled him. The noise of whistles and hooters hurt his ears.

Faces beamed down at him, their mouths scarlet and their noses shiny with happiness. "Hello, Mum and Dad," he said sadly.

"Happy birthday, my boy!" cried Dad, squirting a fountain of water from the flower in his hat.

"Isn't it wonderful, Charley?" giggled
Mum, producing a real egg from his ear.

"You're off to Clown School tomorrow.
I bet you can't wait."

"No, Mum." said Charley gloomily,
staring at the presents. *Please don't make
me open them yet,* he thought.

"Go on, son. Open them now," laughed
Dad, tripping expertly over his own feet and
smiling at Charley. His parents were always
smiling. They were The Merry Muddles –
the two best clowns in the whole history
of the circus.

Charley sat down on a wonky chair and unwrapped his first surprise. The box was long and thin and heavy. He knew exactly what it would be. His new school shoes.

"Try them on, love," said Mum eagerly. "We've got to make sure they don't fit."

They didn't. They were ridiculously large, with red and purple stripes and curly laces. "Thank you," murmured Charley, picking up a small parcel. He shook it. It rattled softly. His first red nose. It smelt of rubber and it pinched.

"Thank you," groaned Charley in a strangled voice, as he tore the wrappings from his baggy trousers, his super-stretch braces, his patchwork shirt, his tiny hat and his sparkly revolving tie.

"And there's a proper professional bucket, too," wheezed Grandma from her corner. She was wearing a silver suit with pom-poms and a tinsel wig. "Belonged to your Gramps that did. He would have been so proud to see you today, Charley." And she hung a string of plastic sausages round his neck.

Charley was ready. There could be no turning back.

"We Muddles have always been clowns," said Dad, after Charley had been officially dunked in the cake. "And we always will be. It's in the blood, son. The greasepaint, the sawdust, the silly walk."

"Yes, Dad," sighed Charley, wiping cream off his patchwork shirt. You see, he loved *watching* the clowns. But he didn't want to *be* one.

Chapter Two

Bright and early the next morning, Mum pressed a paper bag into Charley's hand and pushed him down the caravan steps to wait for the school bus. He heard it long before he actually saw it. The frosty air filled with rattles and bangs and rude popping noises.

"Hop in, lad," chuckled the driver,
"I can see you're keen to get started."
He nodded admiringly at Charley's
dented bucket. Then he tugged
a lever and the bus
chugged away on
its square wheels,
with bubbles
pouring out of
the exhaust pipe.
Mum was waving
a hanky as big as a
tablecloth, but
Charley didn't
notice. He was too
busy dodging the
outsize boots that
blocked his way.
When he finally sat
down, the cushion
crumpled under his bottom
with an embarrassing hoot. Everyone cheered.

PARP.

"Welcome to Clown School," said a voice beside him. "Got your egg?"

"Egg?" said Charley. "No. I've got my lunch box. And my *Cooking For Clowns* book. But I didn't know I needed eggs."

His partner snorted. Charley couldn't tell if it was a boy or girl underneath all that face paint. "You're not going to eat it, silly. You're going to give it to the Clown King. And when you've passed all your exams, you'll be allowed to decorate it."

"For Easter?" Charley was more
confused than before.

"For yourself. For always. Didn't your
parents tell you? As soon as you're a real
clown, you paint your circus-face on an egg.
And no one else is allowed to copy it.
Not ever."

"Oh," said Charley, reaching into the paper bag his mum had given him. "I've got my egg," he added miserably. "It's smashed."

Yellow goo dripped from his fingers, and his new friend shrieked with delight.

"You're a natural. What a brilliant start. My name's Bobo."

By the time the bus reached the school tent, Charley knew all about Bobo.

She was the daughter of a ring master and a trapeze artist, and she'd wanted to be a clown ever since she fell off her first tricycle. "My sisters laughed and that was it," she said. "Being funny is the best thing in the world, isn't it?"

18

"Mmmm," said Charley, who hated making a fool of himself. The other children charged away to their classes, but Bobo led him to the Clown King's office.

"I'll see you later, Charley," yelled Bobo, as she cartwheeled across the circus ring. "We've got cookery this morning. My favourite subject."

Charley was just wondering what his family would say if he ran away from the circus, when a cheery voice called, "Enter, young Charley. We have great hopes for you, my boy."

Charley entered and carefully placed his soggy bag in a bin marked 'Feed Me'. It burped.

"My egg," he began, "I'm awfully sorry sir, but..."

"Excellent, excellent." The Clown King
was a little man in elephant-sized trousers.
He wore a crown made from twisted
balloons, and his shoes squeaked whenever
he moved. On his five-legged desk lay a
rubber pencil, a plastic ink-blot and a
Clown School shield.

"See this?" The Clown King jumped down from his stepladder and peered up at Charley through a bendy telescope. "It's the school motto: 'Make 'em Laugh'. Remember that and you'll never go far wrong. A circus is nothing without its clowns."

With that, he handed Charley a huge L-plate and sent him off to join Bobo's class.

Chapter Three

It was the worst morning of Charley's life.
He couldn't do a thing wrong. His custard
pies weren't runny enough. His cakes
weren't burnt enough. His plates of jelly
weren't wobbly enough. And he simply
couldn't splatter the teacher at all.

"Come on!" shouted the clown cook, waggling his enormous white gloves in the air. "Hit me! Hit me!" But Charley missed. Every time.

"Never mind," said Bobo, as they set off for games. "The first day is always the trickiest. You'll soon get the hang of things."

But Charley wasn't so sure. While the other learners crashed into each other perfectly on the trampoline, or tumbled off the trapeze with their feet frantically pedalling the air, he could only manage a few neat forward rolls.

"No, no, no," wailed the clown acrobat, walking backwards off a bench and catapulting herself into a tank full of feathers. "Straight lines simply aren't funny, Charley Muddle. Now let's see how you balance a tray."

The tray was full of glass bottles. Charley took it nervously and crept towards the obstacle course. The teacher groaned and banged her head against the bouncy wall of the tent.

"Careful clowns are not comical, Muddle," she said. "Show him, Bobo."

Bobo twirled the tray on one finger, stumbled over boxes, almost toppled off a see-saw, wobbled horribly across a bridge and skidded past the finishing line. Nothing had fallen or broken.

Then she took a deep bow, and Charley saw that the bottles were glued to the tray.

He was speechless for a moment. Then he started to clap and cheer. "That was incredible, Bobo," he laughed. "You really..."

The room was utterly still apart from him. He looked around. Everyone was staring at him. "Sorry," he whispered. What had he done wrong?

"We are not here to laugh," said the teacher icily. "We are here to create laughter. Go and practise bumping into the door. Fifty times."

Chapter Four

Bruised and miserable, Charley ate his sandwiches sitting on the floor of the food tent. He didn't want to join the others on a long bench. He knew he would be expected to fall off and he just couldn't face it.

"Come on, Charley," said Bobo kindly, slipping on a banana skin and earning herself a gold star. "I'm sure you'll enjoy bucket drill."

But he didn't. He dived out of the way when it was his turn to be showered with silver paper. He hated throwing water at the others. And he was far too polite to balance his bucket over the teacher's door.

Bobo, of course, was hilarious. And
although he tried very hard, Charley couldn't
help laughing when she got her bottom
jammed in her bucket and scampered round
the arena like a tin tortoise. "That's *so*
funny," he howled, mopping his eyes with
a corner of his shirt. "That is *so funny*."

The clown tumbler was not amused.

"Cheer up, Charley," said Bobo. "That's
the great thing about being a clown. It
doesn't matter if you go wrong. Just as
long as you..."

"Make 'em laugh," sighed Charley. "Yes.
I know."

"How did it go, son?" asked Dad eagerly when Charley arrived home. "How many stars did you get? I expect you'll win the Clowning Cup at the end of the year. The Muddles always do. I can't wait to see you standing on that stage, shaking hands with the Clown King and squishing him with the champion's custard pie."

"Yes, Dad," said Charley, pulling off his baggy uniform and putting on his comfy grey play-clothes. What else could he say? He didn't want to upset his family. They were all beaming at him, their faces full of pride.

So day after day he caught the school bus.
Day after day he did his best to enjoy the
gunge battles, the fake snake chases, the
crazy-car driving lessons. But the only thing
he really liked was watching Bobo and the
others. That was why he was always getting
into trouble for giggling and cheering.

When he took home his end-of-term
report, he crept off to bed early and buried
his head under the pillow. He couldn't bear
to see the painted blue tears under
everyone's eyes. The upside-down smiles.
He was sure he had failed all his clowning
tests. Plate spinning, funny falls, silly cycling,
the lot.

And it was prize day tomorrow.

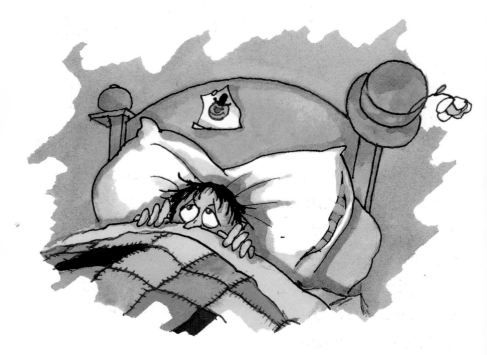

Chapter Five

Charley sat beside Bobo and watched the teachers play musical chairs on the stage. The circus band played party tunes and behind him he could hear the parents gossiping. He wondered if Mum and Dad and Gran had bothered to come, but he didn't look round.

Today all Charley's friends were wearing their full make-up. Each face was different, but each was funny in its own way. And when the children received their Clowning Certificates, they could paint their eggs and become part of the Clown School success story.

Charley alone was bare faced. His red nose would never stay on properly, and the greasepaint gave him spots. "Never mind," said Bobo. "Who needs make-up when you've got a real smile?"

There came a whisper of excitement.
The Clown King tripped up the steps and
sat on the ceremonial whoopee cushion.
The trumpets blared, a hush fell, and the
prizes were awarded one-by-one while the
parents cheered themselves hoarse.

At last, only two learners remained in their seats.

"And now," said the Clown King, "for this year's Clowning Cup. And it goes, as I'm sure you've guessed, to Bobo. An outstanding clown, who will bring fame and fortune to the sawdust ring for many years to come."

"Well done," whispered Charley to his friend. "You deserve it." And he laughed louder than all the rest when Bobo splattered the Clown King with her custard pie.

Make 'em Laugh

Once the Cup had been presented, the parents began to fidget. They were ready to go home. But Charley sat very still while the other clowns paraded around the ring. He felt terribly lonely. What would become of him now? Another year in the learners' class? Another year of failure?

"Ladies and gentlemen, boys and girls," announced the Clown King. "Just before the final fanfare, I have one more name to mention. You see..."

He twizzled his nose thoughtfully, "I've always said that a circus is nothing without its clowns. 'Make 'em Laugh,' that's my motto. But I've forgotten about the most important people of all, haven't I?"

The parents looked at each other. Everyone was puzzled. Particularly Charley.

The Clown King went on. "I've forgotten the audience, my friends. Where would a circus be without someone to clap and cheer and shout for more? I'll tell you...

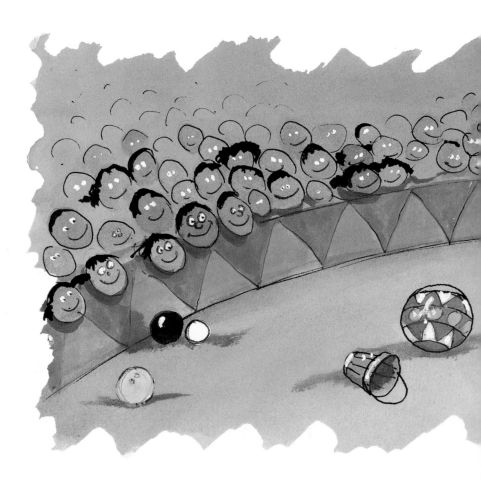

Nowhere, of course. And that's why
I'm presenting a very special trophy today –
to The Best Audience in the World. Step
forward, Charley Muddle!"

Charley stood up and stared in
amazement. His clown friends had formed
an archway of tickling sticks. Bobo led him
through the fluffy tunnel, and as he took his
prize from the Clown King, the big top
thundered with applause.

"We want Charley," everyone chanted.

"Three cheers for Charley," yelled Bobo.

"For He's a Jolly Good Fellow," played the band.

"That's our Charley," sniffed Mum, dabbing her wet eyes with her tablecloth-hanky.

"I always knew he was a winner," croaked Dad.

"His Gramps would have been so proud," agreed Gran with a happy sigh.

Back at Boring Street Junior School, Charley showed his award to all his old friends. It was magnificent. A pair of silver hands on springs, forever clapping and waving.

And whenever the circus came to town, there was Charley, in the front row, cheering for Bobo and laughing so loudly he made everyone else want to laugh, too. Not a failure at all, but a Very Important Person indeed.

Look out for more titles in the Super Stars range:

Superheroes Down the Plughole by Keith Brumpton

Elasticman, Mothgirl and the others have lost their powers...
When they learn that the Superhero Inspectorate is coming
to check them out, the pressure is on. Can our clapped-out
crew of caped crusaders prove once and for all that they really
are still superheroes?

Long John Santa by Chris Powling

Long John the Pirate is too old and achy to be a buccaneer any
more, but all the local job centre can offer him is a job as Santa
at the local department store. Every day, the queues to see Long
John Santa get longer and longer – they are soon so long that the
real Santa arrives to see what all the fuss is about. He's not happy
to find that Long John is becoming more popular than him...

You can buy all these books from your local bookseller, or order
them direct from the publisher. For more information about
Super Stars, write to: *The Sales Department, Macdonald Young Books,
61 Western Road, Hove, East Sussex BN3 1JD*

47